Sophie

Sophie

Mem Fox

ILLUSTRATED BY

Aminah Brenda Lynn Robinson

A TRUMPET CLUB SPECIAL EDITION

ISBN 0-590-06581-5

Text copyright © 1994, 1989 by Mem Fox.
Illustrations copyright © 1994 by Aminah Brenda Lynn Robinson.
All rights reserved. Published by Scholastic Inc., 555 Broadway, New York, NY 10012, by arrangement with Harcourt Brace & Co.
TRUMPET and the TRUMPET logo are registered trademarks of Scholastic Inc.

12 11 10 9 8 7 6 5 4 3 2 1   7 8 9/9 0 1 2/0

Printed in the U.S.A.   14

First Scholastic printing, January 1997

The paintings in this book were done in acrylics, dyes, and house paint on rag cloth.
The display type was set in Gorilla and the text type was set in Leawood Book by Thompson Type, San Diego, California.

Designed by Lydia D'moch.

For Frank Hodge
— M. F.

In memory of my father
— A. B. L. R.

Once there was no Sophie.

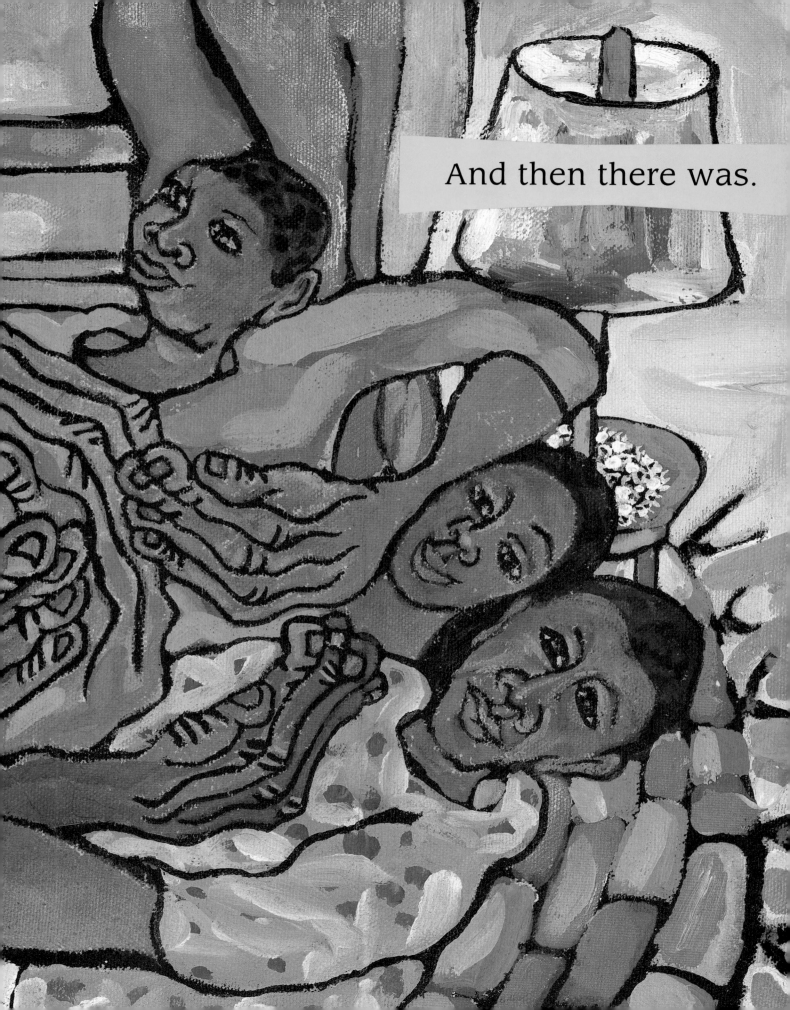

And then there was.

Sophie's hand curled round Grandpa's finger.

Grandpa and little Sophie loved each other.

Sophie grew

and grew

and grew

till she was big enough

to work with Grandpa,

big enough to look Grandpa in the eye.

Grandpa grew older

and slower

and smaller.

Sophie and little Grandpa loved each other.

Grandpa's hand held on to Sophie's.

And then there was no Grandpa,

just emptiness and sadness for a while,

till a tiny hand held
on to Sophie's

and sweetness filled the world, once again.